THE BERWICK BEAR & HIS FIDDLE

Cara Lockhart Smith

SERAFINA PRESS

For Arianne and Lamar

Published in Great Britain by
SERAFINA PRESS
The Smokehouse Gallery
St Ella's Place
Eyemouth
Berwickshire
TD14 8HP

ISBN 0-9552696-0-1

First published in Great Britain in 2006

Printed in Great Britain by Martins the Printers, Berwick upon Tweed
www.martins-the-printers.com

The bear travelled from a long way off, carrying his fiddle in its case. It was all he had in the world.

He came to a town by the
sea. Outside the Town Hall
he began to play his fiddle.
For a long time he played in
the heat of the sun.

Then the bear grew
weary. He lay down
and closed his eyes.
He meant to doze,
but soon he was fast
asleep.

Along came a boy and his sister. The boy liked the look of the fiddle.

He picked it up and ran off down the road.

All of a sudden, the bear
woke up. He roared with
pain when he found that
his fiddle had gone.

The bear and the girl set off to hunt for the fiddle.

They ran down West Street, over Bridge Street, and came out above the Quay.

Down on the Quayside they found the boy but not the fiddle.

He'd swapped the instrument for a five-pound note from Mrs Robson.

They found Mrs Robson, but HORRORS ! She'd swapped it for a big fish.

"The fisherman's taken the fiddle to give to his girlfriend who lives in the lighthouse,"
said Mrs Robson. "Let's go!" said the sister.

They all jumped into a boat ....

.... and set out over the water.

When the fisherman got to the lighthouse his girlfriend was angry because he was late. She threw his fish and chips at him out of the window.

The fisherman propped the fiddle against the wall to stop it getting greasy. This was a BIG MISTAKE !

For when the boat with the bear and the boy and his sister and Mrs Robson arrived at the lighthouse, the fiddle had GONE !

"Hey look!" said the boy. "That girl in pink has taken the fiddle!"

So the bear ran after the girl in pink, and the boy and his sister and Mrs Robson and the fisherman and his girlfriend came running after.

Some people out for a stroll were walking towards the lighthouse.
When they saw the bear chasing the girl, they tried to stop him.

In the struggle the bear fell SPLAT into the sea.

When he managed to clamber out ....

...the people said: "SORRY ! We didn't know you were searching for your fiddle."
"Look out, the girl in pink is getting away!" shouted the boy.

So they all went chasing after the girl in pink. They chased her back along the pier ....

.... over the sea strand ....

.... over the beautiful wasteland ....

.... and back out on to the Quay. But the girl in pink just kept on getting away. Then the boy caught sight of her peeking out of the Sallyport.

They ran down the Sallyport and up Eastern Lane, and there at last was the girl in pink, just standing and smiling. "I was only teasing," she said, and held out the fiddle, BUT ....

... just at that moment, down swooped a gull and seized the fiddle. Up and away it flew, on to the roofs where it had its nest. The bear climbed a tree and swung himself over to the rooftops.

Now he was high up over the moonlit town.
In the distance he could see his fiddle dangling
dangerously in the air, BUT ....

.... just as the fiddle started to fall, the bear stretched out and caught it in his paws. Then he started to slip down the roof. "HANG ON !" cried everyone from far below. They found a ladder and pushed it up to the bear.

The bear climbed down, holding carefully on to his fiddle. The bear was happy. And the
mother of the boy and his sister was happy too, because she had been looking for them all
over town, and now she had found them.

Then they all went back to the Town Hall and had
a celebration. There was feasting and dancing,
and the bear played his fiddle all night long.

At last, when the music and feasting and dancing were over, the bear gave a bow. Then he sauntered away, across the old bridge, into the shadows of the night.